Everybody Feels...
WORRIED

Moira Harvey
& Holly Sterling

D0493313

Quarto is the authority on a wide range of topics.

Quarto educates, entertains and enriches the lives of our readers—enthusiasts and lovers of hands-on living.

www.quartoknows.com

Author: Moira Harvey
Illustrator: Holly Sterling
Designer: Mike Henson
Editor: Carly Madden
Consultant: Cecilia Essau

© 2020 Quarto Publishing plc
This edition first published in 2020
by QED Publishing,
an imprint of The Quarto Group.
The Old Brewery, 6 Blundell Street,
London N7 9BH, United Kingdom.
T (0)20 7700 6700 F (0)20 7700 8066
www.Quarto-Knows.com

A catalogue record for this book is available from the British Library.

ISBN 978-0-7112-5046-8

Manufactured in Guangzhou China EB052020
9 8 7 6 5 4 3 2 1

Contents

Feeling worried

Everybody feels worried sometimes.
You might get the feeling if...

...you're about to go on a trip to somewhere new.

...you're going to have to stand up in front of lots of people.

WORRIED

...something big is going to change in your life.

...you have a school test or a sports game coming up.

...you think something bad might be about to happen to you.

How it feels

Everything's sad,
as though it's raining
inside your head
and soon it will leak out
in your tears.
Sniff... you are feeling...
worried.

Ava feels worried

It was the day before
my school trip.
I had so many worries
I couldn't sleep.

Who will look after me?
What if **I** need help?
What if **I** get lost?

What if? What if? What if?

My worries were thoughts
like noisy monsters that jumped
around and kept me awake.

"Have you got worry monsters? Tell me all about them," said Dad. So I did.

"Let's make some new thoughts to push out the old ones," said Dad.

The school trip isn't very far from home.

There will be teachers there to look after you.

You can ask your teachers for anything you need.

It should be fun and you'll have lots to tell us when you get home.

My new thoughts got rid of my old ones.
The worry monsters disappeared!

Noah feels worried

It was the day of my
school football match.
I felt so worried I couldn't
eat my breakfast.

What if **I** didn't play well?

What if **I** messed up?

I felt so worried that I didn't want
to play in the match any more.

"I don't want to go to school,"
I said, and I started to cry.

14

"Let's talk about what made
your tears," said Mum,
so I told her.

"I want to be great in the
football match, but what if
I'm not?" I said.

"I think you will be good and this is what will happen..." said Mum. Then she pretended to be me playing football.

"Here comes Noah. He scores!"

It was fun to imagine being good in the match. I started to look forward to it instead of worrying about it.

On the day of the match I played really well, just like we imagined I would.

Goal!

Feeling better

Ava and her Dad talked together about her worries, and why they wouldn't happen in real life. Ava was able to make them disappear.

Noah and his Mum imagined good things happening to him in his football match. It helped him worry less and play well, too.

Ava and Noah both talked to
someone about their worries
and that helped them.

Ava's story

 1 Ava couldn't sleep because she was worried about her school trip.

 **2** Her worries were like noisy monsters. She told her Dad about them.

 3 Ava and her Dad made some new thoughts to push out the old thoughts.

 4 It helped Ava to go to sleep.

Noah's story

1 Noah was very worried about playing in a football match. He wanted to play really well, but what if he didn't?

2 The worry put him off playing and he cried.

3 He told his Mum why he was upset.

4 His Mum helped him imagine playing well at the football match. It helped him worry less and enjoy the match, too.

Story words

awake

When you are not asleep. Being worried can keep you awake.

change

When things don't stay the same. Change can make you feel worried because things may be new and different.

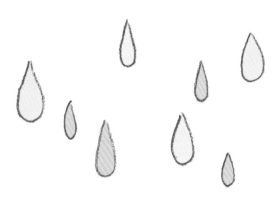

disappeared

When something has gone away. Ava's worry monsters disappeared in the story.

imagine

To think of something happening in your head. Noah imagined good things happening in his football match.

leak

When water comes out of something.

new thoughts

New ideas. You can think up new ideas to replace old ones.

old thoughts

Ideas you once had. You can change them.

pretending

When someone makes up a story and acts it out. Noah and his Mum pretended to be playing in the football match.

sometimes

When something happens, but not all the time.

talk

Speaking to someone. It helps to talk to someone about your worries.

thoughts

Thoughts are ideas in your head. Ava had thoughts about her school trip that were worrying her, such as "What if I get lost?"

what if?

A question about what might happen. Thinking about 'what if' questions can make you feel worried.

What if?
What if?
What if?

Next steps

The stories in this book have been written to give children an introduction to feeling worried, through events that they are familiar with. Here are some ideas to help you explore the feelings from the story together.

Talking

- Discuss how Ava felt. She was worrying about what might happen on her trip.
- Discuss how Noah felt. He wanted to do really well at his football match, but was worried he might fail.
- Talk about how Noah and Ava overcame their worried feelings. They both felt better when they talked about their worries and began thinking differently.
- Look at page 4. Everybody is worried sometimes. Talk about times when children might feel this way. Can your child think of times this has happened to them?
- Talk about how feeling worried makes people behave. Ava couldn't sleep and Noah burst into tears.
- Look at the poem on page 5. You could help your child to write their own poem about what it's like to feel worried.

Make up a story

On pages 20-21 the stories have been broken down into four-stage sequences. Use this as a model to work together, making a simple sequence of events about somebody feeling worried and then feeling better. Ask your child to suggest the sequence of events and a way to resolve their story at the end.

An art session

Do a drawing session related to the feelings in this book. Here are some suggestions for drawings:

- A worry monster.
- The unhappy crying face of someone who feels worried. The happy face of someone who isn't feeling worried.
- Noah playing football or Ava enjoying her school trip.

An acting session

Choose a scene and act it out, for example:

- Ava and her Dad making her worry monsters disappear.
- Noah and his Mum pretending to play in a football match.